# THE ADVENTURES OF ABIGAIL
## And Her Ball

### By
# NOELLE TATE
## Illustrated By Mike Paige

ISBN-13: 978-0-578-62335-1

Union, NJ

Edited by Susan Burlingame
Interior Design by Tami Boyce (tamiboyce.com)

# For **ABIGAIL**

Thank you for bringing tremendous joy to my life.
Until we meet again.

Do you know Abigail?
She is the happiest dog in town.


Abigail is a very beautiful Bichon Frise.
She loves to wear a purple scarf and
a small pink bow in her hair.


Hmmm. Let's see.
Where is Abigail?
Do you see her?

Oh, there she is!

Shhh! Abigail is sleeping.

Can you whisper?

Just like always, she is sleeping
right next to her favorite toy.

Abigail's favorite toy is a ball.
But not just any ball!
It is a ball with a toy penguin inside!

Abigail loves her ball.
Can you think of a
name for the
penguin?

Oh! Abigail is waking up from her nap.

First, she stretches and yawns.
She opens her mouth wide when
she yawns and sticks her tushy
in the air to stretch.

Can you stretch and yawn with Abigail?

Next, Abigail picks up her ball
and brings it to her dish.
Her breakfast is ready for her hungry tummy.
She eats all of her food and
drinks her water like a good girl.

Abigail eats a very healthy breakfast.
Her favorite toppings are carrots and watermelon!
Do you have a favorite breakfast?

Abigail is scratching on the door.
She must want to go outside.

Mommy opens the door for Abigail on this nice summer day.

"UH OH!"

Abigail's ball rolls out the door and bounces down the sidewalk.

Mommy says,
"Go fetch your
ball, Abigail!"
as Daddy peeks
out the door.

Abigail begins to
run after the ball.

Boing!

Boing!

Boing!

The ball bounces down the sidewalk
and all the way into town!
Abigail is careful to stay on the sidewalk.

Abigail's ball bounces past her neighbor
and Abigail barks a hello to the
puppy next door, "Woof, woof!"

"Ruff, ruff!" the puppy
answers saying,"Hello!
I hope you catch your ball!"

The ball bounces by the bakery.
Rico, the baker, throws Abigail a homemade dog bone made of oats, honey, and peanut butter.

Abigail stops chasing the ball long enough to catch her delicious treat.

"Woof!!!" barks Abigail who is so happy to have such generous friends in the neighborhood.

"Good girl, Abigail!" says Rico.
"Now go get your ball!"

The ball bounces through the post office door.
Arthur, the local postmaster,
looks at Abigail and smiles.

"Sorry, Abigail!" says Arthur.
"No dogs allowed in the post office."
Arthur likes Abigail very much,
but he has to follow the rules!
He throws the ball outside
for Abigail to chase again.

WOOOOSH!

Abigail licks a stamp for a
neighbor on her way out the door.
The neighbor says, "Thank you!"

The ball bounces
right by Veronica, the pet groomer
who cuts Abigail's hair.

As Abigail runs by,
Veronica shouts, "Wait, Abigail!
You lost your bow!"

Abigail does not hear her
and continues to run.
She is too busy chasing her ball
to worry about her pink bow.
She will have to find it later!

Abigail chases the ball and jumps so high
over some children playing on the sidewalk.
Their names are Ted and Debbie.
The children wave. "Hi, Abigail!" says Ted.

"Come out and play once you
catch your ball!" Debbie yells after her.
"Woof! Woof!" barks Abigail happily.

The ball bounces through the yard of the town's
animal shelter that saves dogs and pets just like Abigail.
Abigail watches as the ball hits the shelter with a

right over the heads of one rescue dog,
two bunnies, and three chickens!
Will you name all of the animals?

Abigail loves to play with the rescued pets
and is so happy when her new friends are adopted.
She knows the adopted pets are so lucky, just like her.

Then, the ball bumps into a fence with a

and bounces down the sidewalk.

Here she goes again!
Abigail must be getting tired.

Finally, the ball rolls and stops at a door
that Abigail knows very well.

Abigail picks up the ball with her mouth
and the door opens.

"Abigail! What a nice surprise!"
says Abigail's grandma.

Abigail happily runs into Grandma's house!
She loves Grandma because
she spoils her with love and good food.

Grandma sits in her favorite chair,
and Abigail jumps up into her lap.
Grandma pets Abigail and they both smile.


Abigail is tired from running and chasing her ball.
Grandma's lap is a perfect place for a nap!


When Abigail wakes up again,
she will have to find her bow!

What an adventure today
for Abigail and her ball.

The Adventures Continue...

# Meet the AUTHOR and ILLUSTRATOR

AUTHOR NOELLE TATE was born and raised in New Jersey. She is grateful to have had Abigail as her best friend for almost 18 years and this book was written in honor of their friendship. Noelle and her husband, Karl, recently rescued a Shih Tzu and Maltese mix who they named Lanie Lou. Noelle is also a director, actress, and singer, and when she is not using her beloved creative side, she is running her own bookkeeping business. She loves to garden, cook, and spend time with her family and friends.

Find Noelle at www.noelletate.com.

ILLUSTRATOR MIKE PAIGE and Winston live in Medfield, Massachusetts. Mike works at an afterschool program with K-1 students. In his spare time, he makes woodburned Christmas ornaments.

Winston is a standard Schnauzer that loves going hiking. In his spare time, he sleeps on the furniture.

Find Mike on Instagram @mikepaigestudios.

# THE REAL ABIGAIL

## THANK YOU

I wish to thank my husband, Karl Hammerle, for his support in publishing this book that is near and dear to my heart. Thank you to my illustrator, Mike Paige, for bringing this to life exactly as I had imagined and to my graphic designers, Brittany Cooper and Christine Camarda, for working magic when I needed it. Special thanks to my brother, Michael Tate, for giving me the tools to design this book, and to my parents, Arthur & Deborah Tate, and my grandparents, Americo & Theodora LaSalvia, for bringing Abigail into my life. And thank you for reading this book—I would love to hear from you and would be happy to read your review!

Made in the USA
Middletown, DE
20 January 2020